D1126136

TIME FOR FUN

with Elmo and Friends!

Storybook Treasury

Published by Dalmatian Press, LLC, 2012. The DALMATIAN PRESS name and logo are trademarks of Dalmatian Press, LLC, Franklin, Tennessee 37067. 1-866-418-2572

Printed in China
ISBN: 1-61524-670-3

12 13 14 15 ZY 38144 10 9 8 7 6 5 4 3 2 1

20221

By Emily Thompson • Illustrated by Tom Leigh

1
One tire . . .

. . . makes a swing.

2

Two pieces of bread . . .

. . . make a sandwich.

3

Three snowballs . . .

. . . make a snowman.

4

Four letters . . .

. . . make Elmo's name.

5

Five musicians . . .

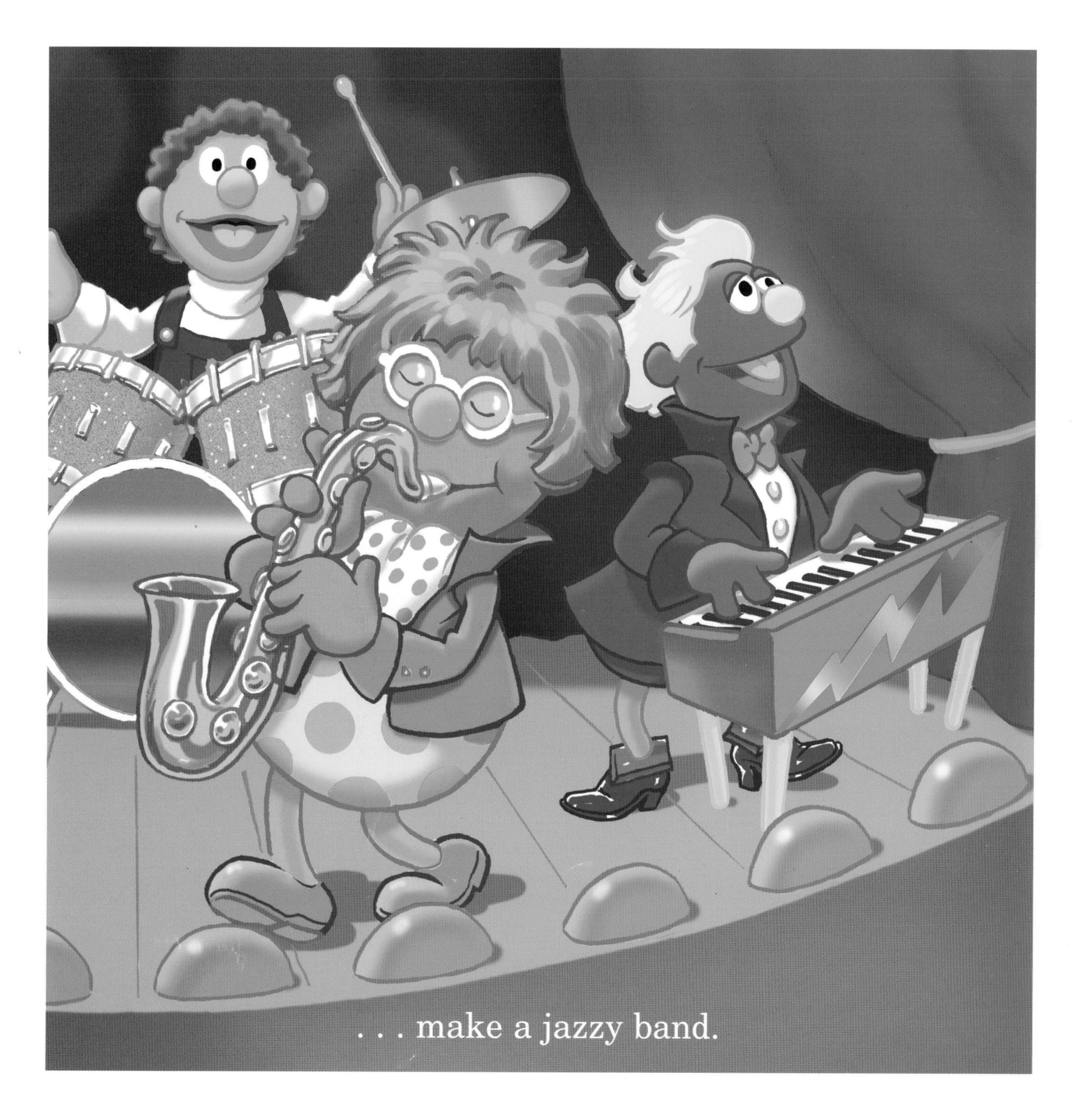
. . . make a jazzy band.

6

Six friends make a pyramid.

7
Seven stars make the Big Dipper.

8

Eight patches . . .

. . . make Elmo's quilt.

9 Nine baseball players make a team.

10
Ten monsters . . .

. . . make a mess!

The End

By Sarah Albee • Illustrated by Tom Brannon

Shall we dance?
Cha cha cha

Who's the best?
Cha cha cha

Flats and **heels**.
Cha cha cha

Hat and vest.
Cha cha cha

First in line.
Hop hop hop

Here's the **last**!
Hop hop hop

Some dance **slow.**
Bop-de-bop

Some dance **fast**!
Bop-de-bop

Short and **tall**.
Dipsy-doo

Boy and **girl**.
Dipsy-doo

Stop to rest.
Dipsy-phew!

Start to twirl!
Dipsy-woooo!

Many dance.
Shaboom shaboom

A **few** are done.
Shaboom shaboom

Some drink water.

Shaboom shaboom

All have fun!

Shaboom shaboom

So, who's the best . . .
Cha cha cha

. . . out on the floor?
Cha cha cha

We can't be sure.
Cha cha cha

They're out the door!

Cha cha cha

The End

By Sarah Albee and P.J. Shaw • Illustrated by Tom Brannon

ROCCO

It was almost time for Zoe to go to school. She was humming and tapping a spoon against her cereal bowl.

"Zoe, how would you like to go with Daddy to the office today?" said her mother. "It's Take Your Little Monster to Work Day."

"Don't joke me!" Zoe exclaimed.

"It's true," said her father. "You can go to work with me today."

So Zoe said, "Okay!"

"Look at the clothes I picked, Mommy," Zoe said. "I'm not going to wear my tutu today. I'll wear my office outfit instead."

"And a starry necklace!" said her mommy.

"This will be cool!" Zoe said. "We can draw with markers, and Daddy can show me his computer!"

Zoe's mother gave her a kiss. "Good-bye, sweetie. Have a good day with Daddy."

"Whoa, wait a minute. Hold the phone," Zoe said suddenly. "I can't miss school today! We're going to learn about shapes."

"Don't worry," said her father. "Your teacher said it was okay. My office has lots of different shapes. We'll learn about them together."

"When we get there, can I make a paperclip necklace and swivel around in your chair?" Zoe asked her father.

"As long as you're quiet as a mouse," he replied.

"I can be a mouse, Daddy. Hey, I bet you don't know the answer to this," she snickered. "What's a mouse's favorite game?"

"Hide and Squeak!"

After they stopped giggling, Zoe and her father left for work.

When they got to the office, Daddy made a special place for Zoe to sit, right beside his desk.

"That box is made of rectangle shapes," he told her. "Each rectangle has four sides and four corners."

"I like rectangles," said Zoe, "but I like circles better. When is circle time?"

"Grownups don't have circle time," her father explained. "But here's a pencil and some paper so you can draw pictures of circles." He held up the paper. "What shape is this paper, Zoe?"

"I know," she said. "A rectangle! It has four corners and four sides. Two sides are long, and two are short."

"That's right," Daddy said. "You know, a square is a kind of rectangle. Both have four sides, but a square has sides that are all the *same* length."

ZOE

B1510.20

"Is it almost time to go outside and play?" Zoe asked after a while.

"Uh, no, honey," said her father. "Grownups don't have recess. Would you like to fill this cup with water so you can water my plant?"

Zoe nodded and took the cup.

"You can tell your teacher the cone-shaped cup was kind of like a triangle," Daddy said. "Triangles have three sides and three corners."

"Telly says triangles are fas-cin-a-ting," Zoe giggled.

"When is snack time?" Zoe asked, after watering the plant.
Her father was talking on the telephone, so he opened a drawer and handed Zoe a roll of mints.
"Have one of these," he whispered.

The mints were circle-shaped, but they didn't taste as good as the round cracker snacks at school.

Finally, Zoe's father hung up the phone. "Lunchtime!" he said cheerfully.

"Yippee!" cried Zoe. "Show me to the pizza!"

They headed to the cafeteria.

"Well, honey, they're not serving pizza today," said Daddy, helping Zoe with her tray. "Sometimes they serve things in grownup cafeterias that kids aren't used to eating. But just because it's new doesn't mean it's not delicious."

"Really?" said Zoe. She decided to try the tomatoes and broccoli. Broccoli looked like a little tree!

After lunch, Zoe plopped down again at her desk.

"We take a nap at school," she yawned. "But I'm a big girl today. No nap, right?"

"I could use a nap myself," her father smiled. "But you're right. At a grownup job, you don't take naps. Here, why don't you rest and make a paperclip necklace while I go to my meeting?"

Zoe loved necklaces!

So Zoe made a necklace for her mommy and a red rubberband ball for Elmo.

"The paperclips are like little ovals, and the ball is round," she thought. "I'll tell Elmo his ball is shaped like a circle."

Finally, it was time to go home.

"So, how did you like going to work with me today?" asked Zoe's father.

Zoe did a little pirouette. "I don't like the office as much as school, but it was fun being with you. And I found lots of shapes, too!"

"I have an idea," Daddy suggested. "Let's put some pieces of paper, the cup, a paperclip, and the rubberband ball in your box, and we'll take them to school tomorrow to show off what we learned together."

"Thank you, Daddy. We'll be in great shape!" Zoe joked.

When Zoe gave Elmo his ball the next day, Elmo said, "Wow! That's the best rubberband ball Elmo ever saw! Did Zoe like going to the office?"

"It was neat," she said. "I really liked Take Your Little Monster to Work Day. But, Elmo, you know what's *really* cool? When it's time to Take Your Daddy to School!"

The End

PD
123
POLICE
123

Watch Out for Banana Peels

and Other Important Sesame Safety Tips

By Sarah Albee • Illustrated by Tom Brannon

Hello there, boys and girls!
I am Officer Grover, and this is my Safety Deputy, Elmo.
We have some very important safety tips
to tell you about today. Here is the first one!
SAFETY TIP #1:
Be careful
turning the pages
of a book
so you don't get
a paper cut.

Okay, Officer Grover!
Deputy Elmo will be careful turning the page so that we can talk about the next safety tip!
SP
SAFETY DEPUTY

SAFETY TIP #2: Clean up toys and spills that could make someone fall. And watch out for banana peels!
Uh-oh.
CAUTION WET FLOOR

SAFETY TIP #3: Always wear a helmet and safety gear when riding a bike or skating.
And be sure to wear a helmet when you are being shot out of a cannon!

SAFETY TIP #4: **Even when it looks cute and friendly, never pet a strange dog.**

Or any OTHER animal!

SAFETY TIP #5: Be careful when you cross the street.
Always hold a grownup's hand. And look both ways!
WALK

You never know what might be coming!
I like to look UP, too.

SAFETY TIP #6: Hold the handrail on stairs and escalators.
Make sure your laces are tied before you ride!
Try the elevator, sir.

SAFETY TIP #7: Be sure to buckle up!
Especially in outer space!
SAFETY PATROL

SAFETY TIP #8: Be careful in the kitchen!
Stay away from the stove!
Carry scissors with the point down.

Keep hands away from appliances!
Be extra careful washing a spoon!

SAFETY TIP #9: Be careful at the playground.
Don't walk in front of the swings!
Take your time when climbing.

SAFETY TIP #10: Protect yourself from the hot sun.
Wear protective clothing!
Wear plenty of sunblock and put on a hat!
Sunglasses protect your eyes.

SAFETY TIP #11: Be careful near water!
Be sure a grownup is watching you at all times.
Always swim with a buddy.
3FT
5FT
2FT

And NEVER run near a swimming pool.
7FT
10FT

SAFETY TIP #12: Be careful when you eat.
Do not gobble your food. Chew it all up before swallowing.
CITATION
Stay away from babies eating sweet potatoes.

SAFETY TIP #13: Never eat a meatloaf sandwich near a pack of wolves.
Make sure that your food isn't too hot!

That is all we have time for today.
Congratulations! Now you can be a Safety Deputy, too.
Here is a badge. Ask a grownup to help you trace it,
cut it out, and stick it on.
WAIT!
Deputy Elmo has one last safety tip.
Do not leave your safety badge
lying around where someone
might sit on it.
SP
SAFETY
DEPUTY

Unless you are a monster, do not gobble food. No, no, no! Chew before swallow. Yeah, yeah!
COOKIES

The End

ABBY CADABBY'S Rhyme Time

By P.J. Shaw • Illustrated by Tom Leigh

"Lumpkin, bumpkin, diddle-diddle dumpkin,
zumpkin, frumpkin, pumpkin!

As a fairy-in-training, I practice my magic tricks with rhymes—
you know, words that end with the same sound, like **bat** and **cat**!
Rhymes are so fun to find! I know—let's find some rhymes together.
Hmmmm. What words rhyme with . . . **rhyme**?"

Grungy grime!
...and slime.
Climb!
Time!

What words rhyme with **sheep**?
Noisy cars that go "**beep**"!
A ballet dancer's **leap**,
And a trash heap to **sweep**.

What words rhyme with **go**?
I bet that you **know**!
There's a boat you can **row**,
And cars that go ***slooooow***.

FISHY WISHES
Uh, oh!
Look, I'm on tippy-toe!

Let's make rhymes for **purple**!
Maybe birds that go **chirple**?
A big Barkley **slurple**,
Or baby's first **burple**!

What rhymes with **icky**?
Bubblegum that is **sticky**,
A game that is **tricky**,
And dogs who are **licky**.
You think purple's hard? Try orange!
Door hinge?

Which words sound like **zap**?
Fairy wings going **flap**!
And the shoes that you **tap**
To the beat—as you **snap**!

Hi, everybody. We just poofed over from Sesame Street.
What rhymes with **tumble**?
Poor Jack's grumpy **grumble**,
Ginger cookies that **crumble**,
And bees that are **bumble**!
Oh, no—not a-g-a-i-n!

Do some words rhyme with **stick**?
Yes! A house made of **brick**,
A soft baby **chick**,
And a camera to **click**!

Hansel, can't we just ask for directions?
TOURISTS!
Say "cheese"!

What rhymes with **tub**?
Well, there's **scrub-a-dub-dub**,
And a miniature **sub**,
Or one baby bear **cub**!

PARTY ¡FIESTA!
What rhymes with **fiesta**?
I know *la respuesta*:
A basket—*la cesta*.
And *una siesta*!

Rosita told me *la respuesta* means "the answer" in Spanish. And *la siesta* means . . .
Elmo knows that! It's a lunchtime nap!
It's noon. Ernie'd better get here soon.

Did You Know
Did You Know
Elmo will tell Dorothy you said hello!
I didn't know fish could glow. That is sooo magical!

What rhymes with **nose**?
Snuffleupagus **toes**,
A swishy fish that **glows**!
And a slithery **hose**.
Did You Know

What words rhyme with **sloppy**,
Like Oscar's **Jalopy**?
Bunnies all **hoppy**
With ears that are **floppy**.

That's the last time
I give a magician a lift.

And what rhymes with **bug**?
Why, a nice slimy **slug**,
Who's all tucked-in and **snug**—
Or the tiniest **hug**.

Let's find rhymes for **story**!
Like a lion who's **roar-y**,
A monster who's **snore-y** . . .
And space that's **explore-y**!
An itsy-bitsy pajama party! Is that not adorable?

And last, what rhymes with **tabby**?
A blankie that's **shabby**,
A fairy named **Abby**,
And the family **Cadabby**!

Hey, are you still here?
Go make up your own rhymes!
TRASH GORDON SPACE GLORY
TRASH GORDON SPACE GLORY
The End

The Pirate Map

Adapted by Kathryn Knight from the script by Billy Aronson

"Oh, we're off to find treasure," sang Pirate Ernie, "just me and my matey! 'Twill sure bring us pleasure and make us feel greaty! Arrrrr!"

"Uh, Ernie," said Pirate Bert, listening to his radio, "the Pirate Weather Service says a storm is coming right this way."

"Don't worry, Bert," assured Ernie as they pulled the rowboat ashore. "We'll find the treasure and leave before the storm hits."

Ernie started to tie the rowboat's rope to a tree. "After all," he went on, "we have the map handed down from your Uncle *Arrrr*-nold. Arrrr!"

"Arrrr!" agreed Bert. He unrolled the old map to study it.

Suddenly . . .

ZWING!

A monkey swung by on a vine, grabbed the map, and—*zwing!*—swung out of sight.

"Hey!" yelled Pirate Bert. "Give us that map, monkey!"

Uh-oh. Ernie had not finished tying the rowboat. While the pirates darted after the little thief, the rowboat drifted out to sea.

The pirates found the monkey sitting high in a tree—with the map!

"Let us have our map," pleaded Ernie, "and we'll give you anything you want."

Oo-ee-oo-oo-ah.

The monkey slid down and tried on Bert's hat.

"My pirate hat?" asked Bert.

Oo-ee-oo-oo-ah. The monkey pointed to Bert's sword.

Bert gulped. "My shiny sword? Anything else?"

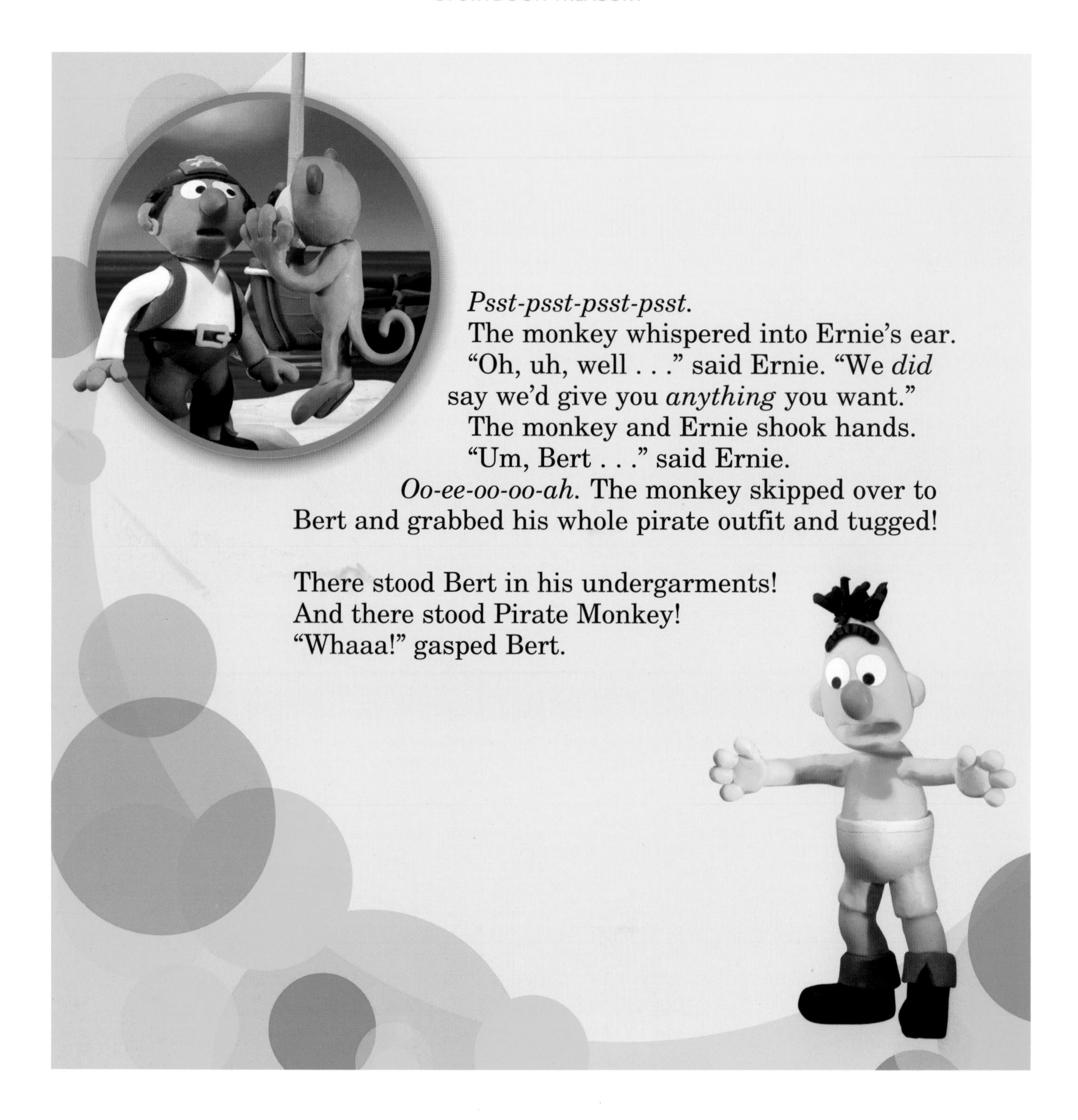

Psst-psst-psst-psst.

The monkey whispered into Ernie's ear.

"Oh, uh, well . . ." said Ernie. "We *did* say we'd give you *anything* you want."

The monkey and Ernie shook hands.

"Um, Bert . . ." said Ernie.

Oo-ee-oo-oo-ah. The monkey skipped over to Bert and grabbed his whole pirate outfit and tugged!

There stood Bert in his undergarments!
And there stood Pirate Monkey!
"Whaaa!" gasped Bert.

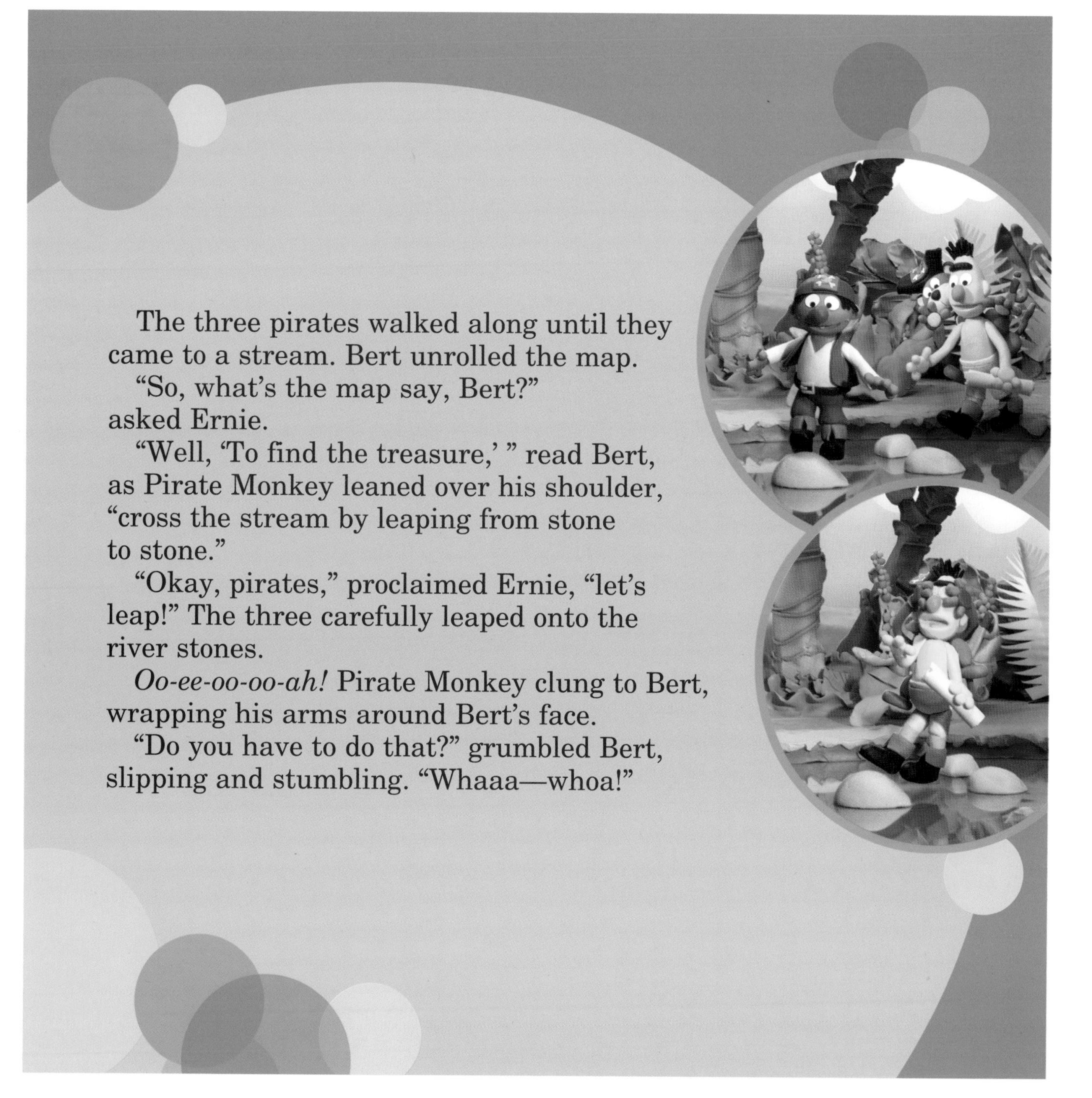

The three pirates walked along until they came to a stream. Bert unrolled the map.

"So, what's the map say, Bert?" asked Ernie.

"Well, 'To find the treasure,' " read Bert, as Pirate Monkey leaned over his shoulder, "cross the stream by leaping from stone to stone."

"Okay, pirates," proclaimed Ernie, "let's leap!" The three carefully leaped onto the river stones.

Oo-ee-oo-oo-ah! Pirate Monkey clung to Bert, wrapping his arms around Bert's face.

"Do you have to do that?" grumbled Bert, slipping and stumbling. "Whaaa—whoa!"

"Ooof!"

Bert fell onto the ground.

Pirate Ernie reached for the map.

" 'Next go three pirate steps to Uncle *Arrrr*-nold's head,' " he read.

Oo-ee-oo-oo-ah! Pirate Monkey pointed ahead to a huge carved head.

"There's Uncle *Arrrr*-nold!" exclaimed Pirate Bert.

"All right, pirates," said Ernie, "take three steps!"

One pirate step! Two pirate steps! Three pirate steps!

"Made it!" cheered the pirates.

Bert unrolled the map and read:

" 'You will find the treasure buried . . . beneath the happy face??' "

"I don't see a happy face," said Pirate Ernie.

Oo-ee-oo-oo-ah! Pirate Monkey slapped his hand onto a happy face on the ground.

"Me neither," said Pirate Bert.

Oops! Pirate Monkey had wiped away the happy face. He took his shiny sword and redrew a happy smile.

Oo-ee-oo-oo-ah!

"The happy face!" cheered Bert and Ernie. "Arrrr!"

Dig-dig-dig-dig-dig-dig-dig-dig-dig!

The pirates dug down until they reached . . .

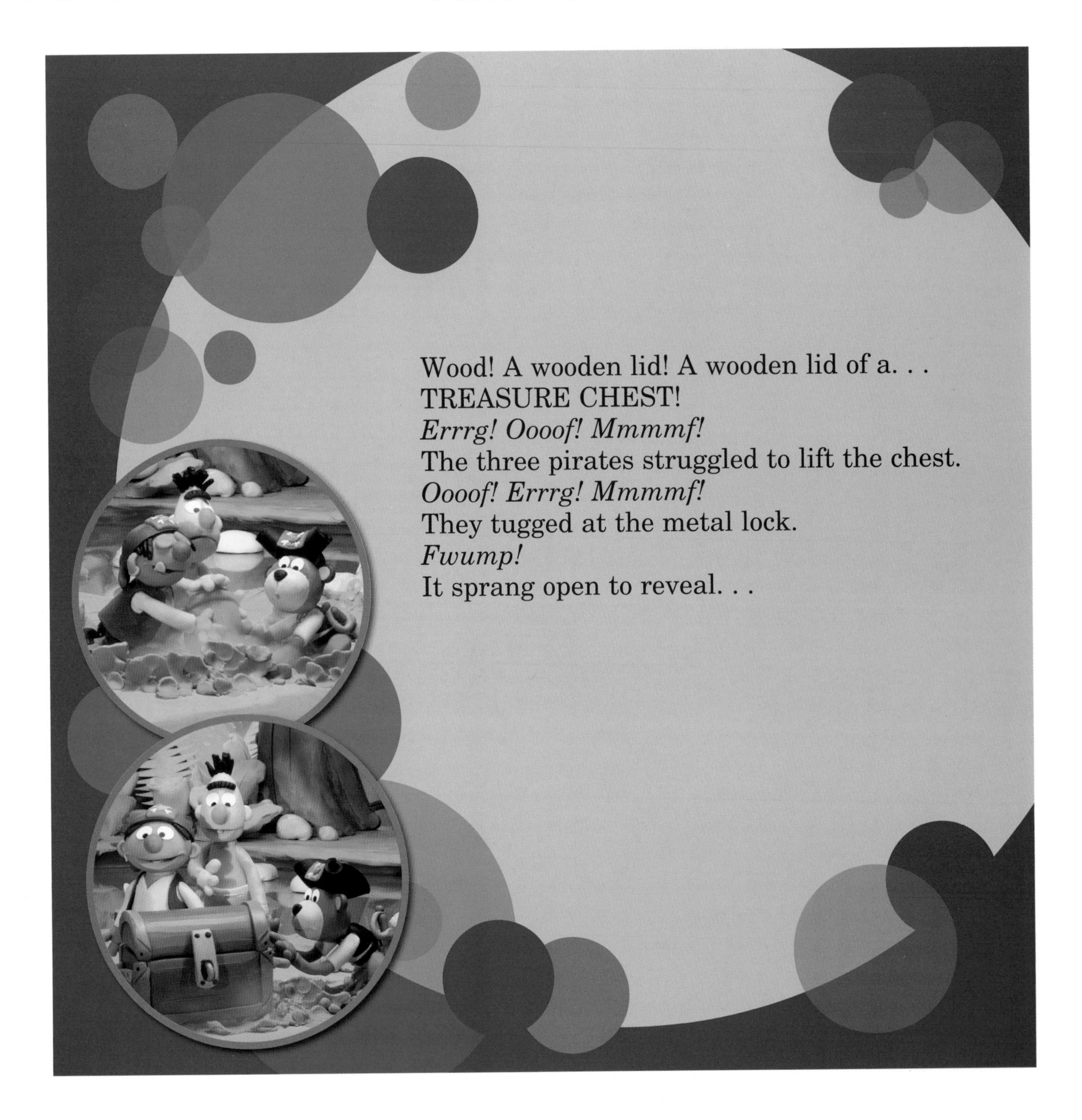

Wood! A wooden lid! A wooden lid of a. . .
TREASURE CHEST!
Errrg! Oooof! Mmmmf!
The three pirates struggled to lift the chest.
Oooof! Errrg! Mmmmf!
They tugged at the metal lock.
Fwump!
It sprang open to reveal. . .

"Socks!" cried Pirate Bert with great delight. He held up colorful socks with happy faces. "Arrrr! What a treasure!"

Pirate Monkey scratched his head.

Pirate Ernie looked puzzled. "What's so great about socks, Bert?"

Bert beamed. "You can never have too many, Ernie."

"To me," said Ernie dreamily, "a treasure would be a chest full of duckies."

Clash! Lightning jagged through the sky.

"Oops! The storm's coming, Bert," said Ernie. "We better get back to the ship!"

Pirate Ernie and Pirate Monkey started to dash away.

"And leave these precious socks?" cried Bert. "No way!"

"We have no choice, Bert," insisted Ernie.

Bert stood firm. "*You* may not give a stitch about socks," he said, "but to *me*, they're as much of a treasure as a chest full of duckies are to *you*."

Ernie smiled.

"Okay, ol' pirate buddy," he said. "If socks mean that much to you, that's good enough for me. All hands on the chest!"

"Arrrr!" they cheered, pulling and pushing the chest to the shore.

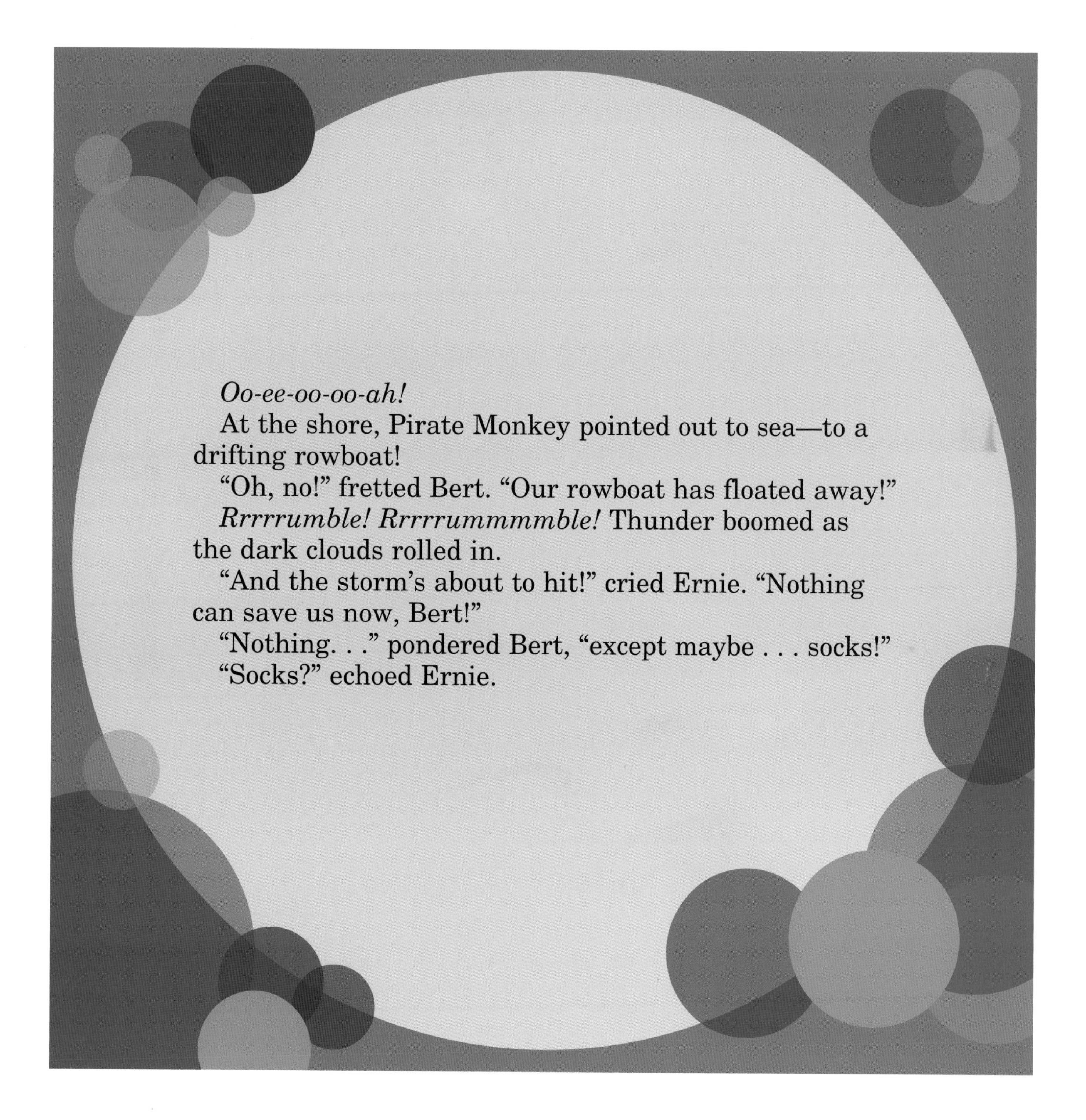

Oo-ee-oo-oo-ah!

At the shore, Pirate Monkey pointed out to sea—to a drifting rowboat!

"Oh, no!" fretted Bert. "Our rowboat has floated away!"

Rrrrrumble! Rrrrrummmmble! Thunder boomed as the dark clouds rolled in.

"And the storm's about to hit!" cried Ernie. "Nothing can save us now, Bert!"

"Nothing. . ." pondered Bert, "except maybe . . . socks!"

"Socks?" echoed Ernie.

"You're right, Bert!" proclaimed Pirate Ernie, admiring the happy-faced sails. "Those socks really were treasure!"

"And now we feel greaty!" sang Bert and Ernie. "We two and our matey!"

"*Arrrr!*" agreed Pirate Monkey.

"Hee hee hee," chuckled Ernie.

The Penguin

Adapted by Kathryn Knight from the script by Luis Santeiro

"Well, Bert, here we are in Antarctica," said Ernie. "Land of ice and snow and . . . *brrrrr* . . . cold!"

"Don't forget penguins," said Bert. "My favorite birds—after pigeons, of course."

"Of course."

Just then . . .

Plip-plop-plip-plop! A small penguin waddled past them.

"Oh! Oh, look at that!" said Bert. "Follow that penguin!"

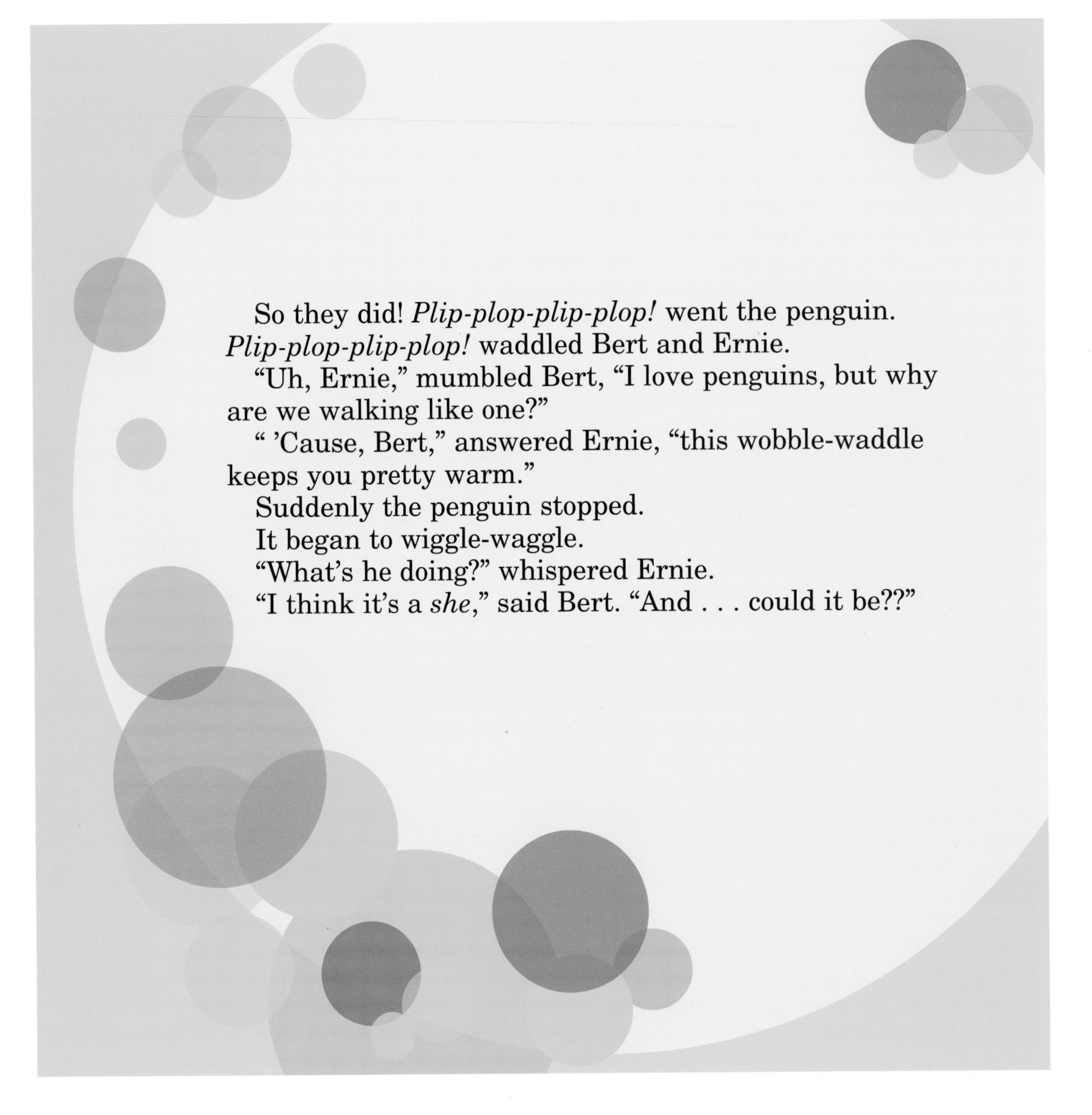

So they did! *Plip-plop-plip-plop!* went the penguin. *Plip-plop-plip-plop!* waddled Bert and Ernie.

"Uh, Ernie," mumbled Bert, "I love penguins, but why are we walking like one?"

" 'Cause, Bert," answered Ernie, "this wobble-waddle keeps you pretty warm."

Suddenly the penguin stopped.

It began to wiggle-waggle.

"What's he doing?" whispered Ernie.

"I think it's a *she*," said Bert. "And . . . could it be??"

Oh, my! An egg appeared!

"It *is*!" cried Bert, leaning closer. "She's going to be a mama penguin! She's hatching an egg! Uh-oh!"

Fwip! The penguin took hold of Bert's parka and—*fwop!*—plopped him right on top of that egg, with a *squawk-squawk-chirp-squawk*.

"Looks like now *you're* hatching it, Bert. Hee hee hee!" snickered Ernie. "And she thinks you speak penguin."

"Sorry," Bert told the penguin. "I only speak a little pigeon. *Ah, coo-coo, coo-coo-coo.*"

But the penguin turned and dove through a hole in the ice.

"Now what?" said Ernie.

SPLASH!

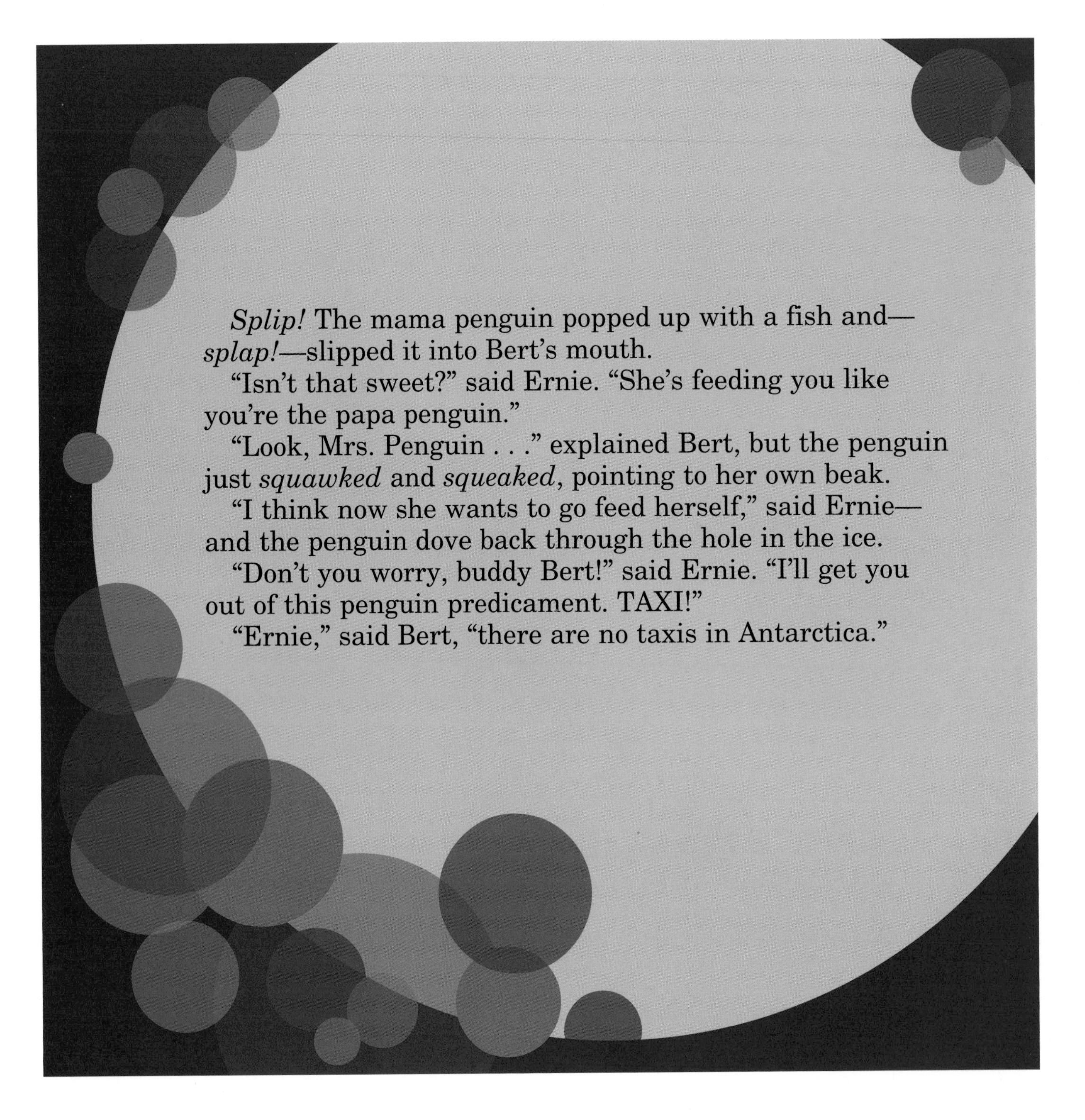

Splip! The mama penguin popped up with a fish and—*splap!*—slipped it into Bert's mouth.

"Isn't that sweet?" said Ernie. "She's feeding you like you're the papa penguin."

"Look, Mrs. Penguin . . ." explained Bert, but the penguin just *squawked* and *squeaked*, pointing to her own beak.

"I think now she wants to go feed herself," said Ernie—and the penguin dove back through the hole in the ice.

"Don't you worry, buddy Bert!" said Ernie. "I'll get you out of this penguin predicament. TAXI!"

"Ernie," said Bert, "there are no taxis in Antarctica."

"Hee hee hee! But there are *dogs* named Taxi!" chuckled Ernie, as a sled dog ran up. "Good boy, Taxi! Come on, Bert! Let's get out of here."

"Wait!" said Bert. "We can't leave this egg. Someone has to keep it warm, or it won't hatch. This egg is . . . Ernie . . . Where's the egg?"

"Oh, no!" cried Bert as they watched Taxi sniff at the egg, pushing it toward—and right over—a cliff!

"Follow that egg!" called Ernie.

Bert and Ernie hopped onto the sled. *Zoom!* They were off, following that egg!

Ga . . . ?
Ga . . . ? Gaa,
gaa, gaa . . . !

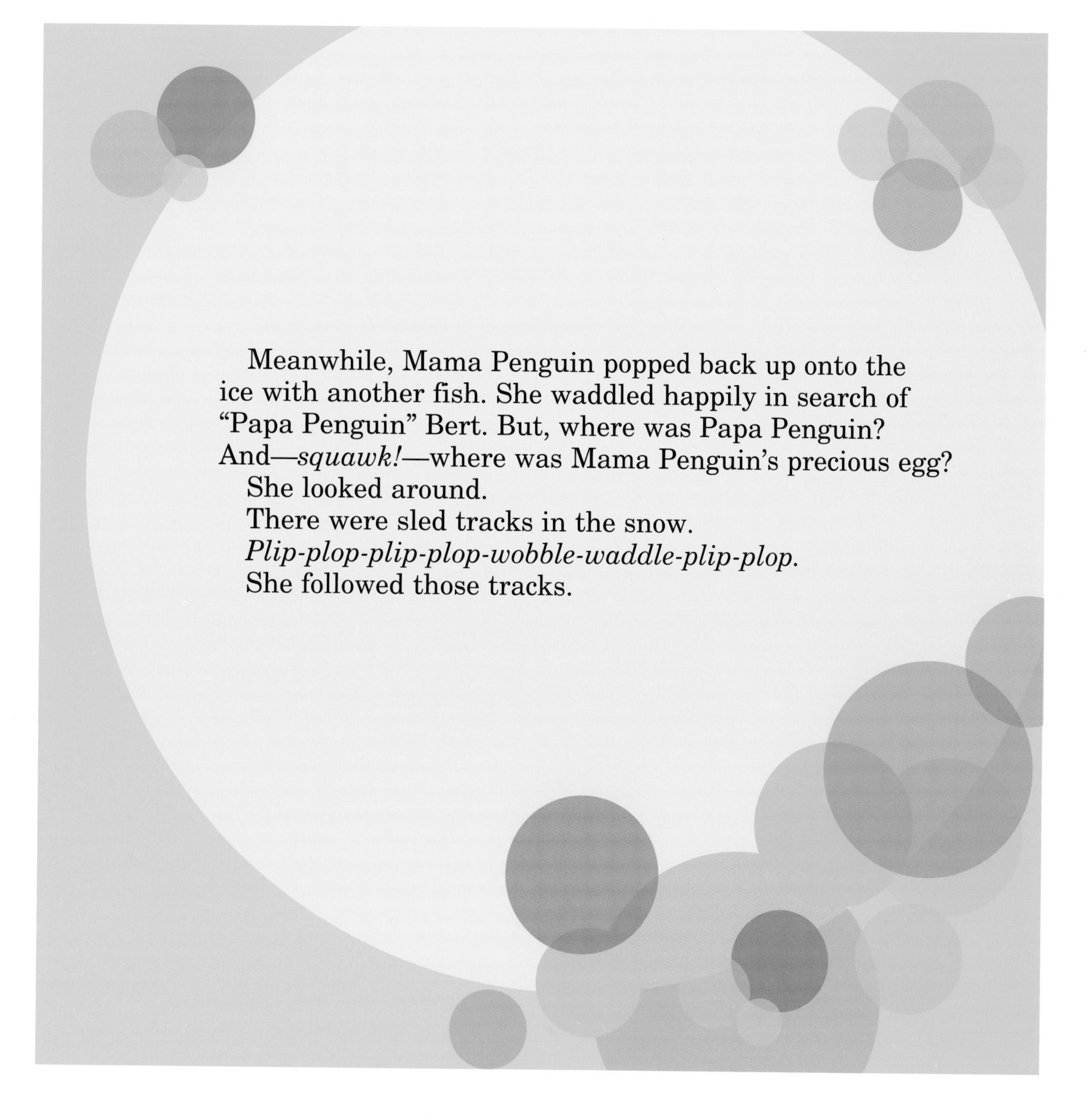

Meanwhile, Mama Penguin popped back up onto the ice with another fish. She waddled happily in search of "Papa Penguin" Bert. But, where was Papa Penguin? And—*squawk!*—where was Mama Penguin's precious egg?

She looked around.

There were sled tracks in the snow.

Plip-plop-plip-plop-wobble-waddle-plip-plop.

She followed those tracks.

"Whew! I'm so glad we caught up with this egg!" said Bert. "Mama Penguin must be worried sick wondering where it is."

"Would you look at Taxi!" chuckled Ernie. "Making snow angels! I think I'll make one, too! Hoo-hoo!"

"Ernie . . ." said Bert as Ernie dove into the snowbank with Taxi. "Ahem! Ernie . . ."

"Stop worrying, Bert. Mama Penguin will find us. She'll be here any minute."

Bert looked down at the egg with a sigh. "Boy, it sure takes patience to be a papa penguin."

CRRRRRRRACK!

"Crack?" wondered Bert.

He looked down. The ice he was sitting on had broken away from the shore! He and the egg were drifting away!

"Oh, no!" cried Bert. "Ernie! Ernieeeeee!"

But Ernie was busy playing.

"Gee, this is so much fun, Bert," he said. "Too bad you can't get off that egg and make a snow angel, too. Bert?"

Ernie looked up to see why Bert didn't answer. Oh, my!

"Bert!" he called. "What are you doing way out there?"

"I'm driftiiiiiiiiiing!" Bert called back.

"Well, don't worry, ol' buddy! I'll save you . . . somehow!"

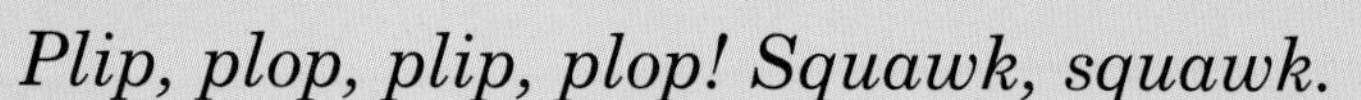

Plip, plop, plip, plop! Squawk, squawk.

Mama Penguin waddled from around the corner. She looked to the right. She looked to the left. She looked up at Ernie. *Squawk?*

Ernie pointed out to the water.

"It's out there," he said, "with Papa."

SQUAWK!!

Ernie looked at the harness and dog reins. He looked at Mama Penguin.

"Well, here," he said, slipping the harness over her head. "Maybe you can use this."

With the reins trailing behind her, Mama Penguin swam out to the floating ice. Bert grabbed hold of the reins and—*hooray!*—Mama Penguin pulled Bert and the egg back to shore.

"Bert!" cheered Ernie, giving him a big hug. "You're safe!"

"Arf! Arf!" agreed Taxi. "Arf! Arf! Arf!"

Bert gave Mama Penguin a big hug.

"Thank you! Thank you! *Uh, coo, coo-coo-coo!*" he said.

"But . . . I am *not* a papa penguin . . . okay?"

"Squawk, squawk, squawk!" squawked Mama Penguin.

Crack!

"Uh, oh," said Bert. "Not *crack* again!"

The little egg wobbled, and—*crrrrack!*—a baby penguin broke out of the egg.

"Squeak!" said the baby.

"Arf!" added Taxi.

"Squawk!" agreed the mama, hugging her baby. Then she placed the little fellow in Bert's arms.

"Awwww . . ." said Ernie. "Look at that!"

"Come here," said Bert softly. "What a cutie. Heh heh heh. *Coo-coo. Oomf!*"

Mama Penguin stuck a fish in Bert's mouth.

"Oh, how sweet!" said Ernie. "That's the penguin way of thanking you for being such a good papa. I hope you're hungry, ol' buddy. Hee hee hee!"

The End

Listen to Your Fish

Terrific Tips for Pet Care

By Sarah Albee • Illustrated by Tom Brannon

Hello there, boys and girls! It is I, Grover, here to tell you my nine "Dos and Don'ts" for taking care of pets!
The most important thing about choosing a pet—whether it is a cute doggie, fish, or llama—is that it should be the right animal for YOUR family. Wild animals LOOK cute and adorable but do not make good pets.
Are you ready for Grover's nine rules for taking care of pets? Turn the page for Rule #1!

Excuse me, sir, but I seem to have lost my sheep.
Leave them alone, and they'll come home.
Mom, she followed me home. Can we keep her?

Pet Rule #1: Do give your pet fresh food and clean water every day.
My first rule!
And do not bother your pet while it's eating!

Hey, no problem, Fluffy.
We can play later.

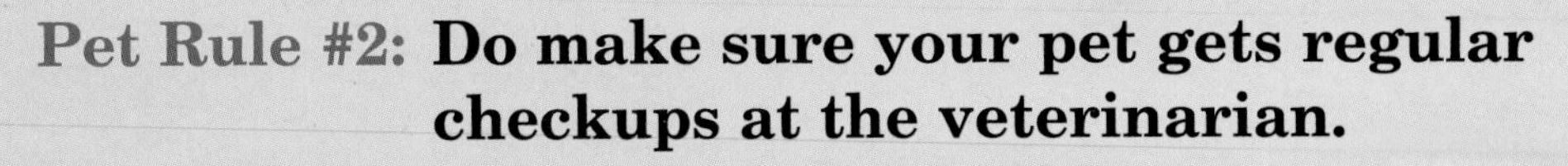

Pet Rule #2: Do make sure your pet gets regular checkups at the veterinarian.

Pet Rule #3: **Do be sure your pet gets exercise every day.**

Pet Rule #4: **Do help your pet stay clean and well-groomed.**

Pet Rule #5: Do not feed pets food from your plate.

It not healthy for them! It teaches pets bad eating habits, like begging for food, which me know is not polite. Oh, look! Cookies for dessert! Gimme, gimme, gimme! Please, oh, please, gimme COOOOOOOOKIES!!!

Pet Rule #6: Do not go near strange dogs . . . or crocodiles.

Pet Rule #7: Do keep your pet on a leash in public places.

Leashes help keep dogs from getting into fights with other dogs.

Pet Rule #8: **Do be gentle with your pet.**
Be sure to watch little babies carefully when they are around pets. Even nice pets might get angry if someone is rough with them.

And remember to wash your hands after you pet your pet.

Pet Rule #9: **Do give your pet lots of love and attention.**

I didn't know where to find you! But you all came home, wagging your tails behind you.

And so, boys and girls, if you remember your friend Grover's nine rules, you will have a happy and healthy pet. Down, kitties! Good kitties. Nice kitties . . .
Pet Rule #10: Do expect a lot of attention from cats after rolling around in catnip.
Maybe you need one more pet rule, Mister Grover.

The End

By P.J. Shaw • Illustrated by Tom Brannon

A
Apple
Abby, Abby, quite Cadabby,
How does your alphabet grow?
With ABC—then letters to Z!
Twenty-six, all in a row.
The alphabet is amazing!
A
B
C
D

B
Bear
Baby Bear, please help Curly with her breakfast.
Bee-Bah!
Here, Curly, eat a banana for your big brother.

C
Cow
Pssst, Jack! Care for some candy beans for that cow?
No, thanks, Lefty! But do you have a candlestick?

Hey, diddle-diddle,
The cat and the fiddle,
The cow jumped over the *moooooon*.
The little dog laughed to see such sport,
And the dish ran away with the spoon.

E
Egg
Look, everybody!
A golden egg!
Extraordinary.
Is it Easter?
Why can't a goose
lay rotten eggs?

F
Frog
Ye Royal Pool
Fair lady, I found this for you.
¡Mi balón de fútbol! Gracias. You are a prince of a frog!

G
Goose
Old Mother Goose,
When she wanted to wander,
Would glide o'er the garden
Upon a grand gander.
Storybook Community School
Goodness gwacious!
Take a gander at that!

H
House
I
Ice Cream
Have some ice cream, Hansel—on the house!
It's Heavenly Honey! Hansel's favorite.
How inviting!

Jog and juggle! Jack, be quick!
Jack, jump over the candlestick!

Old King Cole was a grouchy old soul,
And a grouchy old soul was he.
He called for some junk,
And he called for his skunk,
And he called his kazoo-players three.
K
King
This is kinda kooky!

L
Lamb
DdEeFfGgHhIiJjKkLl
Prairie had a little lamb,
Little lamb, little lamb.
Prairie had a little lamb.
Its fleece was light as snow.
Elmo

Messy Miss Muffet
Sat on a tuffet,
Eating some mud soufflé.
In marched a spider
To sit down beside her—
But she frightened that spider away!

N
Note
Nighty-Night
Nobility
N N
N N
Niceness
Ahh. . .
. . nothing is niftier
than a nightingale's
nocturnal song. . .

O
Oven
P
Pie
Stop that cookie!
PLUM
PEAR
PEACH
OINK!
Oh, oh, oh!
Here I go!
Pat a pie, pat a pie, baker's man.
Make me a pie as fast as you can.
Pat it and prick it and mark it with **P**.
Put it in the oven for piggy and me!

The Queen of Hearts
Made quiche and tarts,
All on a quiet day.
The Knave of Hearts,
He stole those tarts
And quickly ran away!

R
Red
I'm little Red Riding Hood. Who are you?
Elmo is Big Bad Wolf's replacement. He is rappelling with Rapunzel.

S
Star
Sparkle, sparkle, little star,
How I wonder what you are.
Up above the world so high,
Sprinkled in the twinkly sky.
Look, Countess! One star, two stars, three sparkly stars! How stupendous!

T
Tower
U
Up
I could use a friend. Come on up!
Um. . .what a tremendous tower to tackle.

V
Vacuum
Everyone has gone to the palace—*vamoose!* But CinderElmo must vacuum.

W
Wand
Poof! Now CinderElmo can waltz at the ball.
Wow! What a wand!

X
Xylophone
What's so funny about a xylophone or a yo-yo? Y-a-w-nnn. . .
Make the Princess Laugh!
XYZ Xylophones

Z
Y
Yo-yo
Yo! Princess, watch this!

Z
Zipper
Zounds! Four and twenty blackbirds!
Hee hee hee!
Now, that's funny!
Zip it, Ernie.

B is for bye!

Baaa!

The End

By P. J. Shaw • Illustrated by Tom Brannon

"Ow-ow-owooOOO!" howled the Big Bad Wolf one day. "I just want to huff and puff and—and—*blow something in*!" He plopped down on a bench, rubbing his chinny-chin-chin.

"What's wrong, Big Bad?" asked one of the three little pigs.

"I have a tooOOOOthache!" the wolf complained.

"The dentist helps to take care of Elmo's teeth," said Elmo. "Elmo is pretty sure the dentist can help wolf teeth, too."

"That's right," said Abby Cadabby. "My aunt says going to the dentist makes you feel better. And *she's* the tooth fairy, so she should know!"

"Wait! Elmo has an idea," said Elmo. "Abby can do magic! She could make a toothache go away with her training wand."

"I can't *poof* away a toothache, Elmo," said Abby. "I can only turn things into pumpkins. See?" And she waved her wand at a soccer ball: *"Lumpkin, bumpkin, diddle-diddle dumpkin, zumpkin, frumpkin, PUMPKIN!!!"*

Big Bad jumped nervously as the soccer ball turned into a pumpkin.
"Elmo was right," said Big Bad. "I need a dentist—not magic."
"When Big Bad goes to the dentist, Elmo will go with him," Elmo said.

So, the next day, the Big Bad Wolf, Elmo, and Elmo's mommy all went to see Dr. Bradley. In the waiting room, Elmo saw lots of picture books and toys—even an aquarium!

"Ah-oowoooOOO!" Big Bad yowled every now and then.

His toothache was only a teeny bit worse, but he was a wolf and couldn't help himself.

"The dentist will make your tooth better," Elmo's mommy said gently.

"Big Bad Wolf!" called the dental assistant, Miss Stella.
Big Bad whimpered, and Elmo felt worried about his friend.
"We'll take good care of him," Miss Stella told Elmo. "But why don't you come along and keep him company?"

"Good idea!" Elmo agreed. "Elmo can't wait to see how the dentist takes care of *wolf* teeth!"

Miss Stella smiled. "We take care of Big Bad Wolf teeth the same way we take care of little red monster teeth."

"Elmo, let's pretend *you're* having a check-up, so Big Bad can see what happens," said Miss Stella. "Climb up in the dentist's chair and I'll give you a ride."

"Woooo, Elmo is floating," said Elmo, as the chair s-l-o-w-l-y rose.

"Now it's your turn, Big Bad," said Miss Stella.

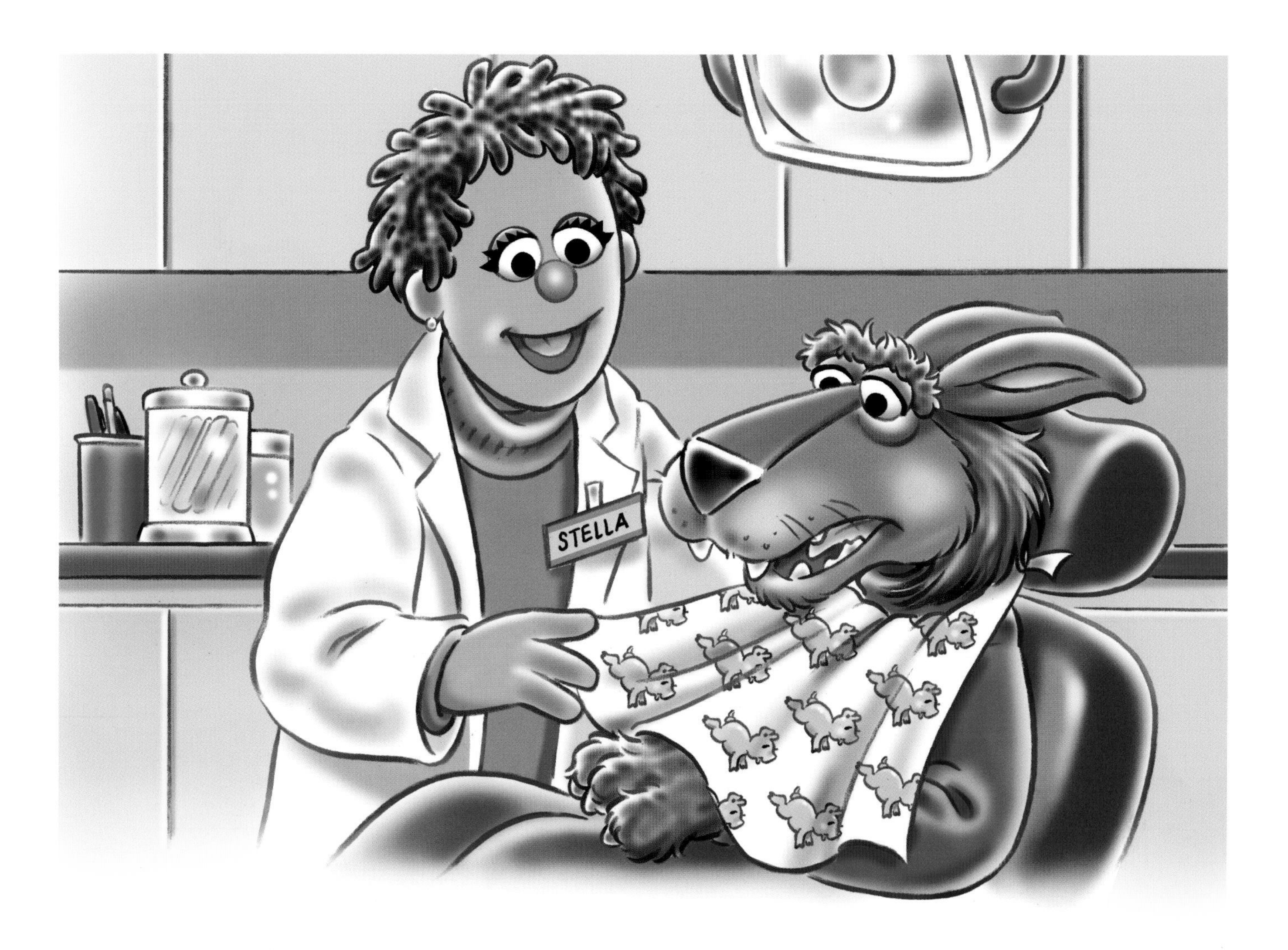

"Will Big Bad get a bib?" Elmo said, remembering his last visit.

"A bib? A baby bib?!" barked the wolf. "Whattaya mean? I'm too BIG! It says so right in my name."

Elmo giggled. "No, silly! It's to keep Big Bad from getting messy when Miss Stella cleans his teeth."

"And *I* wear a mask and gloves to protect little monsters—and big bad wolves—from germs," added Miss Stella.

Big Bad lay back in the chair, and Miss Stella pulled down a light.

"It's pretty dark in there," Elmo said.

"Holy molars!" Miss Stella joked. "What big teeth you have!

"Now," she added seriously, "we take X-rays—little pictures of your teeth. Then we brush your teeth to chase away any sugar bugs."

"*Bugs*?" Elmo exclaimed.

"I mean things like sugar that might start a cavity—a little hole in your tooth. They're not *really* bugs," Miss Stella laughed.

"Ah ew at," mumbled Big Bad. (That's what "I knew that" sounds like with your mouth open wide.)

"Let's pick a yummy toothpaste," said Miss Stella. "What flavor do you like, Big Bad—cinnamon, peppermint, or bubblegum?"

"Ubbleum!" gurgled the wolf with his mouth still open.

"I'll put the toothpaste on this little brush and then we'll tickle your teeth," Miss Stella explained.

"A toothbrush that tickles your teeth. A toothbrush that tickles your teeth!" Elmo chanted. "Just *saying* that makes Elmo feel tickly all over!"

"Feel the brush on your paw—it's very soft," said Miss Stella. "We'll clean between the teeth with skinny string called floss. Then we'll rinse your mouth with a little squirty tool. And, before we're done, we'll look at your tongue and your gums."

"Wow," said Elmo. "That's a mouthful!"

Then Dr. Bradley, the dentist, came in. He gave Big Bad a pat on his shaggy head. "We'll get that tooth fixed right up," he said cheerfully. "Say, Elmo, tell me something: Does a train have teeth?"

"No." Elmo shook his head.

"Then how come it can *CHOO*?!?" Dr. Bradley hooted.

"Woof-woof-woof-woof!" chuckled Big Bad.

"I remember your first check-up, Elmo," said Dr. Bradley. "You were very little. You know, sometimes we even see tiny babies." Then he whispered: "But this is the first time we've ever had a *wolf* in the office."

"Ih mah fuh ahm, hoo," burbled Big Bad, meaning "It's my first time, too."

"My, what big ears you have," Dr. Bradley laughed.

Dr. Bradley asked Elmo to wait outside while he filled Big Bad's cavity. "Don't worry," he told Elmo. "I'll let your friend listen to some fun music while I fix his hurt tooth. How about . . . Wailin' Jennings!"

When he was finished, Dr. Bradley called Elmo back in, and Big Bad proudly showed off his new filling.

“Now, Big Bad, I don’t know what you’ve been eating,” Dr. Bradley said kindly, “but it’s given you a cavity.”

Big Bad looked sheepish.

“So, from now on, be sure to eat lots of yummy, healthy foods, like cereal, vegetables, and fruit.”

“Big Bad and Elmo like bananas!” said Elmo.

"Well, Big Bad, you're all done," said Dr. Bradley. "That filling will stop your toothache."

"Elmo wants to know what happens next, Dr. Bradley," said Elmo.

"Next, we find a time for Big Bad to come back for a check-up. That way, we can stop other cavities before they begin, and he can live happily ever after."

"Thank you, Dr. Bradley," said Elmo.
"Thank yoooOOO!" loudly howled the wolf.
Elmo sighed. "Elmo wishes Big Bad wouldn't do that."

"Here are some new toothbrushes to take with you," said Miss Stella. "And you get to pick something out of the treasure chest."

Elmo picked a wiggly, squiggly, play worm for his goldfish, Dorothy. Big Bad Wolf took a toy tea set for Little Red Riding Hood.

"I'm not bad all the time," he told Elmo's mommy.

"Remember to brush for as long as it takes to sing your ABCs twice, in the morning *and* before you go to bed at night," Miss Stella said.

"Elmo and Big Bad promise," said Elmo. "Good-bye!"

The next day, Big Bad Wolf showed off his fangs to everyone.

"My, what big, healthy teeth you have," said Zoe.

"The better to EAT APPLES with!" Big Bad replied, as the three little pigs scampered by.

"Look out!" they squealed gleefully. "He's after our apples!"

And away they raced—crying "wee, wee, wee," all the way home.

The End

Grover's 10 Terrific Ways to Help Our Wonderful World

By Anna Ross • Illustrated by Tom Leigh

Hello, everybodee! Is this not beau-ti-ful? The world is such a wonderful place! The world is our home. The mountains and deserts, the rivers and lakes belong to all of us.

The world gives us everything we need
to live—food to eat and water to drink
and air to breathe!

The world also gives us snow, sunshine, and rain!

The world takes good care of us, so we must all take care of the world. Oh, I know we can do it!

123
I, Grover, your cute, furry World Ranger, will now tell you ten terrific ways to help our wonderful world.

1
RESPECT
AND BE KIND TO
ALL LIVING THINGS.
Everybody take turns.

Me share cookie crumbs.
Very tasty!

Elmo and Herry are planting a tree.

Ernie plants his seeds in empty milk cartons. When the plants are big enough, he'll put them in a window box.

Bert sorts his brown buttons and shiny paperclips into an old egg carton.

Grouches are great at making treasures out of trash!

Is something broken, I hope?

When Snuffy's sweaters get too small for him,
he gives them to his little sister, Alice.

When Elmo learns to ride a two-wheeler,
he will give his tricycle to Baby Natasha.

Big Bird carries his own shopping bag to the store instead of getting a new bag every time.

Prairie Dawn takes her lunch in a lunchbox instead of in a plastic bag.

Instead of throwing broken things away and buying new things, first see if they can be repaired.

Bert turns off the faucet instead of running the water while he brushes his teeth.

Ernie keeps water in the refrigerator instead of letting the tap run until the water gets cold.

Betty Lou uses cool water instead of warm water whenever she can. It takes energy to heat water.

Cookie Monster closes the refrigerator door quickly so the cold air can't get out. It also takes energy to cool air!

Telly turns off the TV when his show is over.

Are you ready?
1, 2, 3 . . . lights out!
Hah hah!
The Count turns off the lights
when he leaves a room.

9
ALWAYS PUT TRASH
WHERE IT BELONGS.
We'll have this park cleaned up in a jiffy!

10 RECYCLE PAPER, BOTTLES, PLASTICS, AND CANS.

Recycling means using old things to make new things. When we recycle things instead of throwing them away, there is a lot less trash in the world.

I, World Ranger Grover, and my friends take bottles and cans to places where they can be recycled.

We tie up newspapers in bundles and put them out at the curb so the recycling truck can pick them up. Old paper can be recycled into new paper!

Oh, I am so happy!
There is so much we can do to help our wonderful world.

The End

Red or Blue, I Like You!

By Sarah Albee • Illustrated by Tom Brannon

FAIRY TALES

One day in the dentist's waiting room, Elmo made a new friend. Her name was Angela.

When it was time for Angela to go in for her checkup, she asked her father, "Can Elmo come over to our house to play tomorrow?"

Angela's father glanced at Elmo's mother, who smiled and nodded.

The next day, Elmo's mother brought Elmo to Angela's house. When Elmo got there, he couldn't stop looking around Angela's neighborhood.

"Um, Angela?" asked Elmo. "How come all the monsters in your neighborhood are blue? Where are all the different-colored monsters we have on Sesame Street?"

"I don't know." Angela shrugged. "Come on inside! I'll show you my room!"

Elmo and Angela were playing with Angela's train set when her brother, Tony, walked in with some of his friends.

"Hey," Tony said, "do you guys want to come watch *Supermonster* with us?"

"No, thanks," Elmo and Angela said at the same time.

"I thought all red monsters *loved* that show!" Tony said.

"No," said Elmo. "Elmo prefers to play with trains."

"I hope you like spaghetti, Elmo!" said Angela's mother at lunch time.

"It's Elmo's favorite," said Elmo.

"So you red monsters like a lot of the same stuff we blue monsters do, huh?" asked Tony. "I thought all red monsters liked to eat was, you know, red-monster food."

"Red monsters like all kinds of food," said Elmo. "Except maybe brussels sprouts."

Elmo's mother came to pick him up.

"Can Angela come over to Elmo's house tomorrow?" Elmo asked her.

"Well, we'll be having our family reunion. But she is welcome to come!" his mother replied.

So the next day, Angela went to Elmo's house.

"Hi, Angela!" said Elmo. But Angela wasn't looking at Elmo. She was looking all around.

"This is Elmo's family!" said Elmo. "Everyone, this is Elmo's friend Angela."

"Hi," said Angela in a small voice.

"Hello, Angela," said Elmo's aunt. "Elmo says you love spaghetti, so we will make some especially for you."

"But I like chicken and fruit salad, too," said Angela, pointing at the food on the table.

"Oh!" said Elmo's aunt. "I didn't realize that blue monsters liked that kind of food."

While they were eating, there was a knock at the door, and Zoe came in. “Hi, Elmo!” she said. “I’m just dropping off the book I borrowed.”

“She’s orange, just like your aunt,” said Angela after Zoe had left.

“Mmm-hmm,” said Elmo.

Then Telly popped in. “We’re having a T-ball game, Elmo!” he said. “Come on out and play!”

“He’s pink,” whispered Angela.

“Yup,” said Elmo. “Come on, let’s go play!”

As they walked down Sesame Street, Angela kept looking around. "Wow," she said. "There are all different-colored monsters around here!"

"And birds and grouches and people and some Snuffleupaguses, too!" Elmo said. "And we all live happily together."

Angela played T-ball with Elmo and all of his friends. She hit a home run.

“Hey, everyone!” called Big Bird, running into the park. “There’s a new family moving in across the street! Let’s all go welcome them to Sesame Street!”

Both teams dropped their gloves and hurried after Big Bird.

CE
A

"Wow," said Angela. "This is one cool street you live on, Elmo. Can I come back and play tomorrow?"

"Oh, sure, Angela," Elmo replied. "Angela can come back anytime! All monsters are always welcome on Sesame Street!"

The End

123
SESAME STREET